Undercover Ferret

Oliver hid in a closet until he could hear the dance classes beginning. Then he clipped on Spy's leash and dashed upstairs. Outside the coat room for the senior class, Oliver let Spy loose.

"Bring me," he whispered, hoping the ferret would find Rusty Jackson's knapsack.

Oliver couldn't go into the coat room himself. If he got caught, he'd be in big trouble. But no one would notice the little ferret, rifling around inside.

Oliver stood in the hallway. He pretended he was waiting to use the boys' room.

"Spy," he whispered, "I hope you really learned your new trick, this time!"

OLIVER AND THE AMAZING SPY

MICHAEL McBRIER

Illustrated by Blanche Sims

Troll Associates

Library of Congress Cataloging in Publication Data

McBrier, Michael.
  Oliver and the amazing spy.

    Summary: Oliver enlists the help of his friend's pet
ferret to pull a prank on a blackmailing bully.
    [1. Ferrets—Fiction] I. Sims, Blanche, ill.
II. Title.
PZ7.M4782801   1988   [Fic]   87-13793
ISBN 0-8167-1143-7 (lib. bdg.)
ISBN 0-8167-1144-5 (pbk.)

A TROLL BOOK, published by Troll Associates,
Mahwah, NJ 07430

OLIVER AND THE AMAZING SPY

CHAPTER
1

Oliver Moffitt walked up to the Sawyers' house and rang the bell. "Some people have all the luck," he said to himself.

The Sawyers were the only people Oliver had ever known who had actually won a vacation. It was a trip for four to Disney World. Even though it was the first week in June, and summer vacation wouldn't begin for several weeks, the Sawyers were packing up and taking Oliver's friend Scott and his brother, Jimmy, to Florida. They had to take the trip now, or lose their wonderful prize.

Oliver wondered what it would be like to win a trip. Maybe he would go to Africa and see the wild animals. Oliver Moffitt loved animals. He was the only kid he knew who had a business—pet-sitting. That's why he was at the Sawyers'. For the week while they were away,

Oliver was going to take care of Scott's pet. What would it be? A dog? A cat? A bird?

The door opened, and Scott stood there, smiling. Oliver stared for a moment. "It's a little warm for Scott to be wearing a fur hat," Oliver thought.

Suddenly the hat moved. It turned into a skinny, furry animal with a long neck, and a smile on its face.

"What's *that*?" Oliver asked.

"That's my ferret," said Scott. He took the animal off his head and put him on the floor. "His name is Spy, and he's really smart. He can do all kinds of tricks. I'll show you."

Scott stood up and clapped his hands. "Ear!" he said to the ferret. Spy scrambled up Scott's body, sat on his head, and nuzzled his ear. Then he looked down at Oliver and smiled.

"Here's another trick!" said Scott, handing Oliver some Cracker Jacks. "Go up to my room and hide these wherever you want."

Oliver went upstairs and hid the snacks. Then Scott pointed Spy in the direction of his room. Quickly, the weasel-like animal ran to the room and found all the Cracker Jacks. Oliver laughed as the funny little ferret sat happily chomping away.

"Cracker Jacks are his favorite treat," Scott Sawyer told Oliver. "Spy will do *anything* for Cracker Jacks."

"What's his best trick?" Oliver asked.

"Well, ferrets are good at finding things," Scott said as the boys went downstairs. "They can

crawl through little skinny places to look for things. They can bring you things or leave things. That's how Spy got his name. He acts like a real spy. Watch this."

Oliver watched in fascination as Scott set Spy on the ground. He snapped his fingers twice. "Bring me!" he said to Spy. He aimed Spy toward the kitchen. Spy scurried through the dining room, into the kitchen, and slipped inside a cabinet. A moment later he came back with something in his mouth. He dropped an egg cup at Scott's feet.

"Good boy!" exclaimed Scott. He gave Spy a Cracker Jack. Spy arched his back and bounced up and down with excitement.

"Why did he bring an egg cup?" Oliver asked.

Scott shrugged. "I don't know. He brings whatever he wants. Usually he finds pieces of paper. He can take things places too. Watch this."

Scott pulled a piece of paper out of his pocket. "I'll write a note to my brother." He scribbled, "You're a slob. Clean your room before we leave!" on the paper and held it out to Spy. Spy took the paper between his teeth as Scott ran upstairs and set him on the ground outside of Jimmy Sawyer's room.

Spy zipped around Scott's feet a few times. "Just happy," Scott explained in a whisper. Then the ferret slipped through the slightly opened door. When he came out, his mouth was empty. Oliver and Scott walked down to the living room with Spy.

Moments later they heard Jimmy yell, "I am not a slob!"

Scott laughed. "Spy must have taken the note right to Jimmy."

Oliver was impressed.

Scott showed Spy's special whistle to Oliver. "This is really important," he said. "Spy always answers to this whistle. He might not come if you call, but he'll always come if you blow into this. Put the whistle someplace safe."

Oliver tucked it away in his pocket.

Scott explained about Spy's food. "What he really likes is to catch his own. You know, mice and things. But Spy is pretty easy to please. He likes Kit-T-Fine cat food too. And of course Cracker Jacks, but those are just for treats."

At the mention of his favorite food, Spy spun into action. He curled himself into a little ball, hopped up and down, then slithered out to his full length and began dashing around the living room. He used Oliver as a bridge to get from one side of the armchair to the other. He circled the piano bench, ran back to Oliver, leaped into his lap, and smiled at him.

Oliver smiled back. "He's not really smiling at me, is he?" he asked Scott.

"Nah, it just looks like he's smiling because of the markings around his mouth. But I think he really likes you."

Oliver and Spy smiled at each other again. But Oliver was beginning to wonder—not to worry, of course, but just to wonder—how his mother and Pom-pom, his mother's frisky little Shih Tzu, were going to take to Spy.

Spy certainly had a lot of energy.

*   *   *

"Spy certainly has a lot of stuff," Oliver thought as he struggled down the street later. He was carrying a large wire cage in one hand, and a bag of extra litter, cat food, toys, and Cracker Jacks in the other. A leash was attached to Oliver's wrist; Spy frisked at the other end.

The ferret moved along the sidewalk in a way Oliver had never seen before. He didn't run like a dog or cat. He didn't slither like a snake or hop like a rabbit or crawl like a turtle.

"Really," Oliver said to himself, "this animal ripples."

Oliver stopped to rest for a moment. He sat down on the strip of grass next to the sidewalk, with Spy's things spread out around him. Spy, still on his leash, was running around, investigating. He dashed to the curb and peered over it. Suddenly he jumped back and chattered at something lying in the gutter.

"Silly ferret," said Oliver. Even from where he was sitting he could see that it was just a Popsicle wrapper.

Spy must have realized it too. He approached the paper again and looked at it with his dark, beady eyes. Then he pounced on it, took it in his teeth, and brought it to Oliver.

"Thanks, Spy," said Oliver.

Oliver checked his watch. He would have to go home soon, but he was putting it off. He had a feeling his mother was not going to like Spy. Ever since Oliver brought home an alligator, Mrs. Moffitt had not been so wild about her son's pet-sitting business.

Oliver leaned over and played with Spy for a few minutes. He was laughing at the animal's antics when he realized someone was standing beside him. Spy had climbed onto the person's shoe!

He looked up to see Samantha Lawrence, his next-door neighbor and best friend. She was standing very still. "Um, Oliver? What kind of animal is that?"

"He's a ferret," Oliver said. "Isn't he funny?"

"He's not dangerous, then?" said Sam.

"No."

Sam breathed a sigh of relief.

Laughing, Oliver gathered Spy in his arms. All of his friends had gathered around him.

"Boy, you're in a good mood," said Sam. "You must have forgotten. We're starting those dumb dance lessons this week."

Matthew Farley shrugged his shoulders. "Maybe it won't be so bad," he said.

"Matthew should know," Oliver thought. "His parents are always signing him up for classes. Matthew's life is one big car pool."

"Well, I think dancing will be fun," said Jennifer Hayes. She snapped her purple bubble gum. "Especially if they play lots of Purple Worms songs." The Purple Worms were her favorite rock group. She even had a pair of Purple Worms shoes.

"Um, Jennifer," Oliver said. "This is *ballroom* dancing. Everyone does the waltz and the fox trot and stuff like that."

"What?" said Jennifer. "Ew, yick!"

"Not only that," said Josh Burns, "but the boys have to wear suits and ties. And the girls have to wear dresses and little white gloves." He shook his head. "How could Ms. Callahan do this to us?" Ms. Callahan taught Oliver's class at school. She had gotten the parents to sign up their kids for dancing class to improve their "social graces." Josh sighed. "Instead of working on my computer, I'll be twirling around a dance floor with some dumb girl in my arms."

"Look on the bright side," said Oliver. "At least *we* don't have to wear white gloves."

"Why are all of you so down on it?" asked Kim Williams. "I'm looking forward to dancing. I even have a new outfit."

"It's not the dancing," Sam said. "It's what the other kids will say. I don't want them making fun of us. And they will as soon as they hear we're taking *dance* lessons."

"Wait a minute," said Oliver. "What if they *don't* hear we're taking dance lessons?"

"What do you mean?" Sam stared at him.

"If we don't talk about the dance lessons, nobody will know." Oliver smiled. "So if we all swear to keep it a secret . . ."

"Good idea!" everybody said. "We'll keep it a secret!"

They formed a circle and all held hands. Then, running around, they chanted,

"It's a secret, keep it in.
If I should tell, then punch my chin.
IT'S A SECRET! I WON'T TELL—"

14

"Tell *what?*" asked a loud voice. The kids turned around to see Rusty Jackson, the school bully, standing at the back of the group. He had just rolled up on his bicycle. "Come on. What's the secret?"

Oliver sighed. "Just our luck," he muttered.

"We can't tell," said Josh.

"Otherwise, it wouldn't be a secret," Sam added.

"You guys are really funny," Rusty said. He glared at all the kids. "So, 'mum's the word,' eh, Moffitt?" he continued, poking Oliver in the back. "Well, I have my ways of finding things out."

Rusty smiled his sinister smile, then pedaled away on his bicycle.

"What do you think he meant by that?" Sam asked. She sounded puzzled.

"I really don't know," Oliver answered, "but we'd better be prepared for trouble!"

CHAPTER
2

Oliver rushed home with Spy as fast as he could. He had some special chores to get done—before his mother got home.

He puffed his way down the last block to his house, pushed open the door, and ran up the stairs.

Spy was curious about the new house. His little black nose wrinkled and his whiskers quivered. He sniffed at everything in the room. "Come on," Oliver said. "You can look around after Mom gets home."

Oliver needed two trips to get everything up the stairs. Once Spy's things were in his room, he ran over to his dresser.

His *Encyclopedia of Pets* was lined up on the top, along with piles of paper. Oliver hoped that between Spy's belongings and the messy condition of his room, his mom would never notice that he had *another* house guest inside—a snake named Slither!

Slither wasn't dangerous. He was a garter snake, with brightly colored skin. He lived in an aquarium, with a screen over the top. Slither had his own twig to climb on, and sand to slither around on. After Oliver left him some water and a little snake food, Slither was fine for the day.

Oliver made sure the screen on top of Slither's aquarium was tightly sealed. "If Mom found you wandering around the house, I don't know what she'd do," Oliver said to the snake. "But she'd probably start by killing me. She doesn't like it when I sneak things into the house—least of all reptiles!"

Oliver went to work, unpacking the ferret's belongings. "Well, Spy," he said, "this is your new home." He turned around. "Spy?" he said. "Spy?"

The door was open. "Oh, no," Oliver said. "He snuck out!"

Oliver came charging down the stairs. "Spy?" he called. "*Spy!*" Then he stopped.

Mrs. Moffitt stood in the doorway, staring at the hall carpet. There was Spy, smiling up at her.

"Oliver," Mrs. Moffitt said warily, "what is that animal?"

"It's a ferret," Oliver replied. "I mean, *he's* a ferret. His name is Spy. He belongs to the Sawyers. They're going away, and they need . . ."

". . . a place for him to stay," Mrs. Moffitt

said flatly. She gave him a look. "Oliver, didn't we have an agreement? You could keep up your business—as long as you didn't bring animals into the house. After that alligator . . ."

"He was just a *baby* alligator," said Oliver.

"That baby alligator chewed up every piece of furniture in the living room," Mrs. Moffitt said.

"Spy isn't like that," said Oliver. "He's housebroken and everything. I could keep him in my room. He even has a cage."

"Good," said Mrs. Moffitt.

Oliver looked at his mother. "Does that mean he can stay? It would be only a week."

Mrs. Moffitt sighed. "I suppose so," she said. "I just wish you had asked me. There are some animals I simply do *not* want in my home. No alligators, for one," she said quickly. "And *no* snakes." She shuddered. "If there's one animal I *hate*, it's a snake."

"Um, sure, Mom," Oliver said a little nervously. "Thanks."

"Maybe you'd better take Spy upstairs," said Mrs. Moffitt. "I don't know if I want Pom-pom to run into him yet."

Oliver scooped up Spy in his arms and started up the stairs.

"Are you sure there's going to be enough space for the two of you in your room?"

"No problem, Mom." Oliver hurried up the rest of the stairs. "There's room for all of us."

The next day at school, Oliver's friends whispered mysteriously about their secret. They also talked about Spy. Everyone wanted to come over that afternoon to meet him. "We didn't really have a chance to see him in action," Sam said. "Not after Rusty showed up."

The first to arrive was Sam. Then came Josh.

"Where's Matthew?" Sam asked the boys.

"At karate class," Josh replied. "He says it's great practice for dancing."

Oliver went upstairs to get Spy, when the doorbell rang again. "Sam, will you get that, please?" Oliver called. "Maybe it's Matthew."

He scooped up Spy and ran quickly downstairs. Sam and Josh had opened the front door. But instead of Matthew, Jennifer and Kim were there—and they were shooting angry looks at each other.

Oliver pulled Sam aside. "What's going on?" he asked.

"Jennifer and Kim are having a fight!" Sam answered.

"I thought they were best friends," said Oliver.

"They were," Sam whispered. "Until Jennifer saw Kim's new shoes. They're just like Jennifer's, with purple worms all over them."

"So?" said Oliver.

"So," Sam continued slowly, "Jennifer wanted to be the only one with Purple Worms shoes."

Oliver shook his head. He looked at his feet and at Josh's. They were both wearing Pro-Team running shoes. Matthew had a pair too. So did practically every boy in their class. Oliver decided that he didn't understand girls at all.

He also decided not to worry about it.

"Okay, everybody, this is Spy," Oliver announced.

The kids in the hall turned their attention to the animal in Oliver's arms.

"Oh, he's neat!" exclaimed Josh.

"Yeah," agreed Sam. "Hey, he's smiling!"

"He's cute," said Jennifer.

"Adorable," said Kim.

"Sweet," said Jennifer.

"Dear," said Kim.

"Cuddly."

"A sweetheart."

"FETCHING."

"DARLING."

Sam rolled her eyes. "MAY I HOLD HIM?" she shouted over the noise Kim and Jennifer were making.

"Sure," replied Oliver. "Let me take his leash off."

Kim and Jennifer stopped arguing. "Take his leash off!" cried Kim. "You mean, let him loose? Ew! Ick!"

"He's tame," Oliver explained patiently. "He's a pet. Just like Princess Fluffy."

"He is not like Princess Fluffy," said Jennifer, bristling, "My cat is—"

"Okay, okay," said Oliver. "I just meant that he won't hurt anyone." Oliver placed Spy in Sam's outstretched arms.

Spy lolled on his back and smiled at Sam.

Sam grinned.

"Put him on the ground so you can see how he walks," Oliver suggested. "It's really amazing."

Sam placed Spy gently on the floor in the hall. Kim and Jennifer screeched and ran to opposite corners of the living room.

Spy rippled slowly around Sam's legs. Then suddenly he arched himself into an upside-down U-shape and began jumping back and forth.

"Yikes! What's he doing?" shrieked Kim.

"He's just fooling around," said Oliver. "Don't worry about it. Here, I'll show you his tricks." Oliver turned to Spy. He clapped his hands. "Spy," he said. "Ear!"

In a flash, Spy had scrambled up Oliver's body and was sitting on his head, nuzzling his ear.

Everybody laughed, even Jennifer and Kim.

"What else can he do?" asked Josh.

"Lots of things," replied Oliver.

He was heading for the kitchen to get some Cracker Jacks, when the doorbell rang again.

Oliver and Spy answered the door together, and found themselves face-to-face with Rusty Jackson.

"Do you know how stupid you look with that dumb thing?" asked Rusty.

"He's tame. And he's fun," said Oliver.

"I wasn't talking to you. I was talking to the ferret." Rusty laughed at his joke. "I just wanted to see him."

"Well, you're seeing him."

"I want to come in and play with him."

Oliver didn't trust Rusty for a second. "No way," he told him.

"I'll bet you won't tell me your secret either." Rusty smiled nastily. He waited for Oliver to say something, but all he got was silence. "What if I told your mother you were keeping a snake in your house?" Rusty went on. "I can prove it to her without even going inside."

"How can you prove that?" Oliver asked suspiciously.

"With this." Rusty held out a photograph. It showed Oliver entering his house. He was looking around guiltily, carrying Slither in his aquarium. The picture was very clear. Oliver could see the stripes on Slither's body. Still worse, he could see the brand-new shirt he had gotten just a week earlier. If his mother saw this photo, she would know it was recent. And she would certainly want to check Oliver's room to see if a snake was inside.

"Where did you get that picture?" Oliver asked.

"I took it myself," Rusty answered proudly. "I was hiding in the bushes right across the street."

Oliver felt his stomach turn cold. He gulped. "So, you want to pet Spy?"

"I want to know what you kids are trying to keep secret," said Rusty. "I want you to tell me." He smiled again, even more nastily. "Think about it. I'll give you a week. If you haven't told me by then, your mom gets this picture."

He walked away. "Take it easy, Moffitt. I've got to get to my darkroom."

Oliver watched as Rusty walked away. Then he went back inside his house, closing the door behind him. "Hey, you guys!" he called to his friends. "I think we've got a problem."

CHAPTER 3

"**B**oy, what a creep!" Sam exclaimed when she'd heard what Rusty had done.

"Yeah," said Jennifer and Kim.

"It's his new hobby," Josh spoke up.

"What is?" asked Oliver. "Being a creep?"

"No, photography. He just got two new cameras. One is just a regular-sized camera. But the other is so small, it fits in the palm of your hand. It takes great pictures though—and develops them by itself." Trust Josh to know all about new inventions. "He's been going all over town taking pictures, especially with his little camera. His parents think he's a really great photographer. They've even set up a darkroom in the basement for him. Now he can develop his own pictures."

"He's no photographer," said Oliver crossly.

"He's just a spy. . . . Oh, no offense, Spy," he said to the ferret.

"Who does he think he is?" cried Jennifer. "Sneaking around taking pictures of things no one's supposed to see, and then using them for . . . for . . ."

"Blackmail," said Oliver quietly. "That's the word."

"Why didn't you take the picture and tear it up?" asked Jennifer.

"That wouldn't do any good," explained Josh. "Rusty has the negatives. He could just make more pictures."

But now Oliver was thinking. "What if we got the pictures—*and* the negatives?"

"How are you going to do that?" asked Sam. "They're in Rusty's darkroom. We can't go in there."

"*We* can't," said Oliver. "But *Spy* can."

"Really?" said Kim.

"No problem," said Oliver. "It's one of his tricks. He'll go into a room, and bring things back. I've seen him do it. Now, Josh, you said Rusty's darkroom is in his basement, right?"

"Right."

"Great. I know he's there now. This is perfect." Oliver attached Spy's leash to his collar. "Come on, you guys. We're going to take a little walk."

Oliver and his friends left the Moffitts' house and walked toward Rusty Jackson's. Spy was glad to be outdoors. He rippled and danced ahead of everybody. Once in a while he chattered excitedly.

When they were two houses away from the Jacksons', Oliver whispered, "Cut through the back yards."

As quietly as possible, Oliver and his friends slipped through the back yards to the edge of Rusty's property.

"Now run for it!" Oliver hissed. Keeping low to the ground, he dashed across Rusty's yard and flattened himself against the house next to one of the basement windows. The others followed.

Oliver handed Spy's leash to Sam. "Here, hold on to him for a minute, okay?" he whispered.

Sam nodded.

Oliver edged sideways and peeked in the basement window. The light was on. Oliver could see a washing machine, a dryer, an old Ping-Pong table, a smaller table holding detergents and a pile of clothes, a shelf full of paint cans and jars of nails and screws—and a door with a crooked sign on it that said: DARKROOM, and under that: RUSTY JACKSON, PHOTOGRAPHER/SOLE PROPRIETOR. Dangling on a string from the doorknob was yet another sign: THE PHOTOGRAPHER IS IN.

Oliver moved back from the window and faced his friends again. "He's in there right now. So we'll have to wait."

"Wait for what?" Kim asked.

"For Rusty to leave. Shhhh!" Oliver said.

The door to the darkroom opened, and Rusty stepped out and stared at a photograph in his hand. He looked very pleased with himself.

Oliver waited until Rusty took the sign off the doorknob and went up the stairs.

"Okay, now," Oliver said to the ferret. Then he took off Spy's leash and put him down by the window. He aimed Spy at the darkroom door. "Now, Spy," he said. *"Bring me!"*

Spy wiggled through the partly open window. Oliver squinted to see where the ferret was going.

"How do you know Spy will go to the darkroom?" Sam asked.

"I know Rusty," Oliver said. "He's the junk-food king of Bartlett Woods. And what's his favorite food?"

"Cracker Jacks," replied Sam instantly.

"Right," said Oliver. "And they happen to be Spy's favorite food too. So, when he smells them . . ."

All the kids crowded around to watch Spy. But Oliver pulled them back. "If Rusty comes back, I don't want him to see us," he hissed.

"How does Spy know what to do?" asked Sam worriedly.

"He's smart," said Oliver. "He just knows. I just hope Rusty's got a good supply of Cracker Jacks in his darkroom."

"Are you sure Spy will come back?" asked Kim.

"Positive," replied Oliver, and he dropped a handful of Cracker Jacks onto the window ledge. "It's part of the trick."

But after several seconds had gone by, Oliver and his friends heard the door to the darkroom open and close.

Oliver and Josh glanced at each other.

A minute went by. Then two more.

Oliver dared to peek in the basement.

Nothing.

"Where is he?" Josh whispered.

Oliver tried to look confident. But inside, he was beginning to get scared. Should he go in and try to find Spy? Oliver knelt by the window, about to open it all the way.

But at that moment, the darkroom door opened and closed again. Seconds later, Spy leaped onto the window ledge, scattering Cracker Jacks all around. He held a lumpy wad of paper between his teeth.

"What is it?" asked Jennifer.

"Is it the negatives?" asked Sam.

Oliver unwrapped the paper. "It's not the negatives, or the pictures," he said. "It's a note or something." He held the paper up, trying to read it. That wasn't an easy job. The note was definitely written by Rusty—nobody in school had handwriting as bad as his. Lots of words had been crossed out or written over.

This is what Oliver saw.

To Dear Dearest Betsy,

~~I tov tike~~ really like
you. I have liked you ever
Since the day I seen you
at the Quik Shopp. I think
you are ~~but if at budital~~
~~beeyoutiful~~ really nice.

I says to myself, "she
is the girl for me." I hope
you think so too. I mean,
that I am the boy for
you. If you do, send me a
not too.

Love,
your friend,
your best speshul friend,

Rusty

"I don't believe this!" Oliver said as he read the note to his friends.

"Oh, *I* do," said Josh, trying not to laugh. "Rusty is in love! And I know who it is. There's a girl named Betsy Hardy in his class. I *thought* he liked her."

"How do you know?" asked Oliver. "Are you sure?"

"Positive. Once I saw him following Betsy home from school. Another time, she tripped and dropped her books and Rusty didn't laugh. Plus, I heard two of his classmates talking about him and Betsy today. They think he has a crush on her too."

"Hey, now it doesn't matter that we didn't get the negatives," Sam said slowly. "You could blackmail Rusty with this, Oliver."

"Yeah." Jennifer giggled. "Make Rusty give you the pictures, or you'll show his note to Betsy."

Oliver looked thoughtfully at the note. "You know," he said, "I think you have an idea there. . . ."

He folded up the note and put it into his pocket. Suddenly, the kitchen light went on.

Sam, Jennifer, Kim, and Josh ran for it.

Oliver grabbed Spy and scampered away from the window. His heart was pounding loudly. He was just about to dart through the Jacksons' back yard when suddenly it was flooded with light!

Oliver jumped into a clump of bushes. He heard voices, but he couldn't make out what they were saying. When he dared to peek through the bushes, he saw Mr. and Mrs. Jackson, standing on the back porch. They looked all around the yard. Then they walked down the steps. Oliver held his breath. They were standing right next to the bush where he was hiding!

"I'm sure I heard something," Mr. Jackson said.

"I know. I heard something too," agreed Rusty's mother.

Oliver held so still, he thought he would burst. He hoped Spy wouldn't chatter or try to run away.

Oliver heard Mrs. Jackson sigh. "Look, dear," she said. "The light's on in the basement. I guess Rusty's in his darkroom again."

"I guess so. Did you see the picture he took of me sitting at my desk?" asked Mr. Jackson. "It's terrific! He really has talent."

"Yes, it was lovely," Mrs. Jackson replied. "But I'm worried about Rusty. He spends much too much time alone in the basement. He ought to be off with children his own age."

Oliver snorted. "Sure," he thought. "But who'd want to be with Rusty?"

At last the Jacksons headed back to the house. "I guess it was just a stray dog, or something," said Mr. Jackson. He and his wife went inside.

The lights went off. Oliver let out a deep sigh. "Come on, Spy." He held out some Cracker Jacks, and clipped on Spy's leash. Together, they took a short cut home.

It was really dark now. The moon was turning yellow and rising above the tops of the trees as Oliver crept across the neighboring yards.

Oliver reached into his pocket to pat the wadded-up love note. "Ha, ha, Rusty Jackson," he thought. "I've really got you now!"

CHAPTER
4

When Oliver got home, his friends were waiting for him. "What happened to you?" said Josh.

"Oh, nothing," Oliver answered. "Rusty's parents almost caught me, that's all."

"You didn't lose that note, did you?" asked Sam.

"Oh, no." Oliver pulled it out of his pocket. The kids all crowded around on the front steps to read the note again. Josh read it aloud, pretending to be Rusty. Everyone was laughing.

"That letter is the funniest thing I've ever seen!" Jennifer had a hand over her mouth to smother her giggles. "If I were Betsy Hardy, I wouldn't know whether to laugh or cry."

"Aw, gee," said Josh. "I think it's 'budifal.' "

Everyone started laughing again.

"I'd love to see Rusty's face when he finds out you have this," Sam said.

"So would I," said Jennifer.

"Me too!" said Kim.

"Well, maybe you can," Oliver said. "I figure on talking to Rusty tomorrow after school."

"We'll be there!" said the girls.

"I wish I could come," said Josh. "But there's a meeting of the computer club."

Oliver grinned. "Well, I'll just have to tell you all about it."

When the group broke up, Oliver went into his house. "Okay, Spy." He unclipped the ferret's leash. "I've got work to do. Want to come with me, or stay down here?"

Spy chattered, then climbed up Oliver's arm, perching on his head.

Oliver laughed. "I guess that means you want to come." Balancing the ferret on his head, Oliver made his way up the stairs.

Pom-pom charged out of Mrs. Moffitt's room, yapping his head off. But when he saw Spy with Oliver, he stopped suddenly and ran back into the room. "Boy," Oliver said to Spy, "too bad we can't keep you here all the time."

Oliver went into his room, and took Spy off his head so he could work. He switched on the radio, and began his pet-sitting chores. It was always a good idea to get them done while his mother wasn't around.

First he peered into the snake's cage. "Hello there, old Slither," he said. "How are you doing? You're going home pretty soon, aren't you? And I've just made sure that Mom will never know you were here."

Oliver checked Slither's food supply. Then he polished the walls of the aquarium. A good pet-sitter always returns his charges looking as clean as possible.

The new Purple Worms song came over the radio. Oliver stopped his work and began to sing along with it. "Oh, baby! My baby!" he sang. "Love is like a worm, a worm . . ." The radio was playing loudly and Oliver was singing loudly. His mother would never allow so much noise when she was at home, so Oliver made good use of the times when she was at her job.

When the song was over, Oliver returned to his work. He went over to Spy's cage, and shook out the rags the ferret slept on. "There you go, Spy," he said. "I've changed your bed for you."

Oliver looked around. "Spy?" he called. Then he gasped.

Spy was leaning up against Slither's aquarium, staring at the snake. He was also poking at the screen on top.

"Spy! Get away from there!" Oliver dashed across the room and grabbed the ferret. "Are you trying to get me into trouble? How can I finish my work if you're going to play with Slither's cage?"

Oliver took Spy downstairs. He quickly checked the first floor to see that there was nothing Spy could get into. Then he put the ferret down, and headed back to his room.

Oliver changed the litter in Spy's box. Then he washed out Spy's dishes and gave him fresh food and water. Just as he finished, he heard his mother come in.

"Hello, Oliver," she called.

Oliver ran downstairs, to see his mother flop into a chair.

"What a day!" Mrs. Moffitt said. "I'm pooped!"

"Can I get you something?" Oliver asked. "A glass of juice?"

Mrs. Moffitt smiled and stretched out her legs. "That sounds good to me."

Oliver ran to the kitchen and poured a glass of juice. When he came back to the living room, he noticed that his mother was sitting very still. She had a funny look on her face.

"Oliver," Mrs. Moffitt said quietly, "what is this animal doing?" She pointed to the top of her head.

"Spy!" Oliver shouted. Sitting on Mrs. Moffitt's head was the little ferret. He had a big smile on his face.

"He's just showing that he likes you, Mom," Oliver tried to explain.

"Oh," Mrs. Moffitt said, rolling her eyes up to see what Spy was doing. "That's just great."

The next day at school, Oliver could hardly wait for his classes to end. When they finally did, he rushed for the bicycle racks. Sam was already waiting for him. Soon, Kim and Jennifer showed up.

"Where's Rusty?" Jennifer wanted to know.

"He should be here soon," said Oliver. "That's his bike over there."

"What's that to you, Moffitt?" Rusty came walking up. He looked at Sam, Kim, and Jenni-

fer. "Are you guys going to tell me your stupid secret?"

"No," said Oliver. "But *you're* going to give me those pictures of me with the snake. And the negatives."

"Oh, yeah?" said Rusty. "And why am I gonna do that?"

Oliver waved the note in Rusty's face.

"Because if you don't, we're going to show this to Betsy Hardy," said Sam, "and she'll find out you can't even spell."

Rusty turned bright red. "Oh, yeah?" he said again. "Well, I was just practicing on that piece of paper. I'm *really* gonna send her a valentine."

"A valentine?" said Jennifer. "But Valentine's Day was months ago."

"I know that," said Rusty. "I thought it would be a neat surprise. She'd never expect it." He turned to Sam. "So Betsy will know that I like her, soon enough. But since you think you're so smart . . ." He began digging around in his knapsack. "See what your friends think of *this*!"

He pulled out a lumpy wad of paper, and handed it to Sam. Sam unfolded it and a picture fell out.

"What on earth?" Sam said. Her cheeks were burning as she looked at the picture. It showed her sitting inside Hulits' Shoe Store. She was trying on a pair of shoes. But not just any shoes. Sam was trying on—

"Purple Worms shoes!" screamed Jennifer. "You too? Did you buy them?"

"Well, I—"

"Did you?"

"Yes," admitted Sam. "I saw yours and Kim's and I really liked them, so I decided to get a pair too."

"You traitor!" shrieked Kim. "We wanted to be the only ones with Purple Worms shoes!"

"You mean, I did!" cried Jennifer. "You're a sneak, Kim. You were supposed to take yours back."

"Well, she's a sneak too," exclaimed Kim, pointing at Sam. "Now everybody's probably going to get Purple Worms shoes."

"Oh, never mind. I'm not talking to you, Kim Williams!"

"And I'm not talking to you, Jennifer Hayes."

"And," continued Jennifer, "I'm especially not talking to you, Samantha Lawrence."

"Me neither," announced Kim.

"Good," said Sam, "because I'm not talking to either of you!"

The girls turned their backs on one another and flounced off to get their bicycles.

Rusty laughed as he watched the girls stalk off. "Nice try, Moffitt." He took the note from Oliver's hand. "Just remember I still have pictures of you. And if you don't want your mom to see them, you'd better tell me what you and your friends are trying to keep secret."

Oliver gulped, but he didn't say anything.

Rusty gave him a hard look. "That's okay, Moffitt," he finally said. "I can wait. At least, I can wait until next Monday. Then your mother will see my pictures."

He grinned evilly and went over to unchain his bike. Seconds later, Rusty pedaled off.

Oliver watched until Rusty had disappeared. "Great," he told himself. "He's still got the pictures, and I'm in even more trouble." Oliver started to head home. "Something tells me I need a better plan!"

CHAPTER
5

When Oliver woke up on Wednesday morning, he was tired. He'd been up half the night, trying to think of some way to fix Rusty. But Oliver was also excited. He had permission to bring Spy to school for the whole day. Ms. Callahan had decided it would be educational for the class to observe a real live ferret.

Oliver jumped out of bed and opened the ferret's cage. "Good morning, Spy," he said. "You have a big day ahead. I hope you're ready for it."

Spy stared at Oliver with happy black eyes.

"Maybe we should run through your tricks once—just for practice," Oliver said. "Ear," he commanded, clapping his hands. Spy scrambled onto Oliver's shoulder and nuzzled his ear.

"Good boy!" cried Oliver. "Now bring me."

He set the ferret on the floor. Spy rushed over to Oliver's pants and dug into the pocket. He came back with a piece of Cracker Jack he had found. Spy chewed on the treat and chattered. He hopped up and down. Then he ran into his cage for a drink of water.

Oliver smiled. "Looks like we're all ready," he said.

Mrs. Moffitt gave Oliver, Sam, and Spy a ride to school that morning. "I hope Spy behaves himself," Mrs. Moffitt said as she stopped the car in front of the entrance to Bartlett Woods Elementary School.

"So do I," replied Oliver.

"Call me at work if you have any trouble."

"Thanks, Mom." Oliver struggled out of the car with Spy's cage. Sam followed, carrying Oliver's books, her own books, and Spy's leash.

They walked proudly up the walk, through the door, and down the hall to Ms. Callahan's classroom.

The first person they saw was Jennifer. Jennifer stuck her tongue out at Sam. Sam made a face at Jennifer. Then Kim came along and made a face at both of them.

Oliver sighed. "Boy," he told himself. "I'm glad boys don't act this silly."

The face-making might have gone on forever, but Ms. Callahan came in. "Well," she said, looking at Spy. "Is this our special classroom visitor?"

Oliver nodded. "His name is Spy Sawyer."

"Why don't you put his cage over there on the science table?" Ms. Callahan suggested. "The students can look at Spy when they come in, and later you can tell us all about him."

"Okay," agreed Oliver.

Sam, Kim, and Jennifer had taken seats as far away from one another as they could find. Oliver sighed. He didn't want his friends to fight among themselves. But he didn't want Rusty to know their secret either. Oliver knew that if he told Rusty, it would be all over the school. He shuddered to think what Rusty and his friends would say.

In fact, when it came down to it, Oliver's one big problem was Rusty Jackson. He was the one blackmailing Oliver. He was the one who got the girls into their fight. "If only we had some way to get back at Rusty," Oliver said to himself. "Too bad going to his darkroom didn't work."

Then Oliver remembered how Rusty had taken Sam's picture out of his school knapsack. That gave Oliver an idea. Maybe Rusty had some more goodies in his knapsack. Maybe Oliver could get Rusty Jackson after all—using Spy!

Oliver could hardly wait to try out his plan. He could pull it off in school that day.

When Spy was settled in his cage on the science table, Oliver's classmates began to crowd around.

Some of the kids thought Spy was cute. They said things like, "Aw, look at him."

And, "Ooh, he's pretty."

And, "Hey, his nose is wiggling!"

Some of the kids thought he was scary. They said things like, "Ew, look at his teeth!"

And, "Oh, gross."

And, "Yikes, are you positive he can't get out of his cage, Oliver?"

A couple of kids actually made fun of Spy. They said things like, "Look at him jump up and down. What does he think he is—a kangaroo?"

And then there was Arabella Jones. She was very smart in science and English. Arabella peered at Spy through the bars of the cage. "A very interesting specimen of the Mustelidae family," she said. Then she looked over at Oliver. "Are you *positive* he can't get out?"

When the bell rang, Ms. Callahan told the students to take their seats. She called the roll. She asked Arabella to lead the class in the Pledge of Allegiance. She spoke to the school principal over the intercom. She collected homework.

Through it all, Spy sat quietly in his cage. He was on his best behavior.

When Ms. Callahan had finished the morning's business, she said, "Class, we have a special visitor today. I think you've all met him. . . . Spy *is* a boy, isn't he, Oliver?"

Oliver nodded.

"And now I'd like Oliver Moffitt to introduce our visitor officially. Oliver?"

Oliver walked over to the ferret cage, opened it, and took Spy out.

Half the class leaned forward for a closer view. The other half screamed and shrank back.

Oliver considered putting Spy's leash on him, but decided not to. Spy could do his tricks better without the leash. Besides, he was on his best behavior.

Oliver held Spy in his arms and walked to the front of the room. "This is Spy Sawyer," he told his classmates. "He's a ferret and he's ten months and two weeks old."

Oliver talked about Spy's habits. He told the class what ferrets eat and what they like to do. Then he asked if there were any questions.

Arabella and Sam raised their hands. Oliver called on Sam. He had a funny feeling he might not know the answer to Arabella's question. Besides, he knew what Sam was going to ask. They had arranged things in the car that morning.

"Yes, Sam?" said Oliver.

"I've heard that ferrets are very smart and can learn tricks. Is that true?"

Kim and Jennifer giggled.

"Why, yes," replied Oliver.

Oliver and Spy demonstrated "Ear" and leaving things. The class was very impressed. Then Oliver set Spy on one of the front-row desks. "What I like about Spy is how well-behaved he is. If I say 'Bring me' to him, he'll—"

The ferret smiled at Oliver. Then he sailed off the desk and headed for the classroom door. Matthew jumped up and reached it a split second before Spy did. He slammed the door shut.

"Thanks, Matthew," said Oliver. But the noise

had frightened Spy. He bolted for the back of the classroom, taking a route between two rows of desks. He ran over Kim's left foot and Arabella's right foot on the way.

Kim shrieked.

Arabella yelled, "Mustelidae on the loose!"

Ms. Callahan shouted, "Oliver, for heaven's sake, put him back in his cage!"

Oliver paused for exactly two seconds to figure out what to do. He could blow Spy's whistle. He could tempt Spy with Cracker Jacks. He could try to tackle Spy.

In the end, Oliver decided the whistle would be the fastest way to get Spy back. He pulled it out of his pocket and blew.

There was a flurry and scurry from under the science table. A moment later, Spy's devilish face appeared. He scampered across the room to Oliver amid a chorus of *ews, eeks,* and *aws.* Oliver rewarded him with a Cracker Jack. Then he fastened Spy's leash to his collar.

"Ms. Callahan," said Oliver, "may I take Spy into the hall for a short walk? I think he's overexcited."

Ms. Callahan looked relieved. "Certainly, certainly," she answered. "Take as long as you need."

Oliver walked Spy out of the room and down the hall. He casually strolled by Rusty Jackson's classroom. As Oliver had hoped, the room was empty. The students were in gym class and the teacher was in the teachers' lounge.

Perfect!

Oliver peered in at Rusty's desk. It was in the front row. Most teachers put Rusty in the front so they could keep an eye on him. Oliver stepped into the room long enough to hold Spy up to Rusty's desk. It smelled strongly of Cracker Jacks.

After Oliver let Spy sniff Rusty's desk, they returned to the hall. Oliver had to be able to keep a lookout for teachers.

The hall was clear. Oliver aimed Spy back into the classroom. "Bring me!" he instructed.

As Oliver had hoped, Spy made a beeline for Rusty's yummy-smelling desk. Oliver kept watch in the hall. A few seconds later, Spy returned with something in his mouth.

An eraser.

That wasn't exactly what Oliver needed. He needed Rusty's pictures—or something that would make as much trouble for Rusty as Rusty had made for Oliver.

Oliver sent Spy back into the classroom three more times. Spy returned with a sock, a pen that wrote in different colors, and a paper airplane. No good.

Oliver had a tough time smuggling everything back to his own desk, but he had no choice. He was afraid to return it to Rusty's. He didn't want to get caught loitering in an empty classroom.

Later that day, when Rusty's class was having recess, Oliver took Spy out for another "walk." He sent the ferret into Rusty's desk five more times. This time he got back a shoelace, a penny,

a comic book, and a spitball. Those were no good. But the last thing Spy brought was perfect. Rusty's report card!

Oliver quickly peeked at it. He counted four F's. And it still wasn't signed. "This is just what I need," Oliver whispered.

He caught sight of Rusty's teacher down the hall and quickly slipped the report card into his pocket. Then Oliver snapped on Spy's leash and returned to Ms. Callahan's room. Now he had only two problems. What would he say to Rusty? And how would he get Rusty's junk back to him?

At the end of school, Oliver, Josh, and Matthew waited at the bike rack for Rusty.

"What do you clowns want?" Rusty said as he came walking up.

"We want those pictures of Oliver—and the negatives," said Josh. "We'll trade them for this interesting report card."

Oliver waved the report card in Rusty's face. He couldn't help gloating a little bit. "Four F's, Rusty. No wonder you were hiding it."

"Hey, I wasn't hiding that report card," Rusty said. "I was going to bring it home tonight. But my desk was all messed up. I couldn't find anything."

He took the report card from Oliver's hand and gave him one of his nastiest smiles. "But since you found it for me, I guess I owe you. So, I'll give you *this*."

Rusty reached into his knapsack. For a second, Oliver thought he was getting his picture. But the photo Rusty handed him was completely different. It showed Josh's house, and two kids in front of it. Josh's back was facing the camera, but Oliver knew it was Josh anyway. The figure was wearing Pro-Team running shoes and the "JOSH" sweat shirt that Josh never let anyone else wear. The other kid was Matthew. He was standing with a bucket of soapy water. Josh held a hose.

But what really caught Oliver's eye was the sign stuck into the ground beside them. It said:

DOGWASH
BEST EVER
LOW PRICES

Oliver's mouth dropped open. Then he frowned. "What's the big idea of trying to horn in on my business?" he said, turning to Josh and Matthew.

"It wasn't my idea," Matthew spoke up nervously. "Josh—"

"Oh, quiet down, Matthew. You're such a chicken." Josh looked at Oliver. "We were just—"

"Who are you calling a chicken, you big fat-head!" Matthew burst out, turning Josh back to face him. "You think you're so smart, bossing people around."

"Fathead, huh?" said Josh. "Why, you—"

Matthew cut him off. "Let me tell you something, fathead. As of this minute, we are no longer friends. You can count me as an enemy from now on." Matthew marched off.

"That goes for me too." Josh started walking away.

"Hey, wait a minute," said Oliver. "*I'm* the one who should be mad. What about this slimy little dog wash?"

Josh turned around. "Well, if you'd let me explain—"

"Why should I listen to an enemy?" Oliver said. "You could have asked me to come in on the dog wash. YOU'RE BOTH MY ENEMIES!" he shouted after them.

"Good!" said Matthew. He marched off.

"Good!" said Josh. He marched off in a different direction.

"Good-bye, traitors," Oliver snarled.

He turned around to march off too. But he bumped into Rusty instead.

Rusty was cackling like a maniac. "Boy, Moffitt. You sure can pick 'em. With friends like those, who needs enemies?"

He laughed again. "What you need is a good pal. Somebody you can tell your secrets to. Somebody like me." Rusty got on his bike. "Unless you want me to tell your secret to your mother." He pedaled away, whistling.

Oliver stood there, his shoulders sagging. "There must be something I can do," he said to himself, "to stop Rusty Jackson!"

CHAPTER 6

Doomsday.

The only thing Oliver could think of that was worse than going to dance class was going to dance class with your mortal enemies at a place called Miss Leslie's Dance Studio for Young Ladies and Gentlemen.

On Thursday afternoon, Oliver hurried home from school. "It's funny to hurry to get someplace you don't want to go to," he thought. But Oliver had to change his clothes before dance class. There were strict rules about what to wear. Each boy had to wear a dark suit, a white shirt, dress shoes that "must be polished," and something called a "conservative tie."

"I don't have any conservative ties," Oliver had mentioned to his mother the night before. "I guess I won't be able to go to Miss Leslie's after all."

"Nonsense," replied Mrs. Moffitt. "All your ties are conservative."

"They are?" said Oliver. He pulled a blue-and-white striped one out of his closet. "Is this conservative?"

"Very," answered his mother. "It'll look perfect with your suit. Now, don't forget to polish your shoes."

"I won't," Oliver had mumbled.

When Oliver got home on Thursday, he took off his school clothes and flung them on the floor. Then he put on the shirt, the suit, his good shoes, and his conservative tie. He was just about ready to leave for Miss Leslie's when the phone rang.

It was Mrs. Moffitt.

"Did you brush your hair?" she asked.

"No."

"Your teeth?"

"No."

"Then do both, please. And slick your hair down."

Oliver hung up the phone. "Oh, gross," he said aloud. But he did what his mother had asked.

At last he said good-bye to Spy, Slither, and Pom-pom and went out the back door of his house. His suit was pressed, his shoes were polished, and his hair was flattened with water. "I sure hope no one sees me," he thought. "I really look like a nerd."

Oliver tiptoed to the corner of his house, peeked around the corner, and ran to the driveway. He hid behind a bush, peered through the branches, and saw that the coast was clear. He ran to the sidewalk. No one in sight. He breathed a sigh of relief.

Oliver was walking briskly down the sidewalk, when suddenly he heard footsteps behind him.

Oliver walked faster.

The footsteps walked faster.

Oliver broke into a jog.

The footsteps broke into a jog.

Oliver began to run.

The footsteps spoke. "Going somewhere, Moffitt?"

It was Rusty.

Oliver stopped in his tracks. He gulped. "Just on my way to . . ."

"A funeral?" Rusty laughed loudly at his joke.

"Uh . . . yes. That's it," said Oliver slowly. "I *am* going to a funeral!"

"You *are?*" asked Rusty in amazement.

"Yes," said Oliver sadly. "Want to come?"

"Oh, well . . . no thanks." Rusty turned around and ran off.

Oliver snickered. "Rusty may be going to his own funeral soon, when he shows his parents his report card." Then he breathed a sigh of relief. "That was a close call!"

Miss Leslie's Dance Studio for Young Ladies and Gentlemen was not very hard to find. It was the place with all the kids hanging around who didn't want to go inside.

In the crowd, Oliver spotted Sam, Jennifer,

Kim, Josh, and Matthew. Each one was standing alone, looking stiff and angry. Oliver decided to go talk to Sam. He had to pass Matthew on the way.

"Jerk," said Matthew.

"Traitor," said Oliver.

He had to pass Josh too.

Josh didn't say anything. He just turned his head the other way.

Sam greeted Oliver with, "Will you look at Jennifer and Kim? They had the *nerve* to wear their Purple Worms shoes."

Oliver looked at Jennifer's and Kim's feet. Then he looked at Sam's feet. "You're wearing yours too," he exclaimed.

"That's different."

"Why?" asked Oliver.

"I don't know. . . ."

"Well," said Oliver, "it's almost four-thirty. I guess we'd better go inside."

"I guess," said Sam.

A few other kids were going inside too. Oliver and Sam followed them. They walked through a fancy hallway and found themselves in a huge room.

"Is this a *ball*room?" asked Sam, wide-eyed.

"No, stupid, it's an airport," said Jennifer as she entered.

Sam made her ugliest face at Jennifer. She pulled her eyes down with her fingers, stuck out her tongue, and snorted like a pig.

"Young lady!" cried a horrified voice.

Sam jerked her hands away from her eyes.

"Me?" she asked. She looked up—way up—into the face of the tallest, sternest woman she had ever seen.

"Yes," said the woman. "Although I'm not sure *young lady* is a fitting term for you."

"Are you Miss Leslie?" Sam whispered.

"I am. And who are you?"

"I'm—I'm Jennifer Hayes."

Jennifer gasped. "She is not! Her name is Samantha Lawrence, and she's a—"

"What, may I ask, are *those*?" Miss Leslie interrupted. She pointed to the girls' feet.

Sam and Jennifer looked at each other.

"They're Purple Worms shoes," said Jennifer.

"Well, they're not allowed in my school. Young ladies are to wear simple black shoes, no heel, strap is optional. The next time you come to class, I expect you to— There's another pair!"

Miss Leslie had just spotted Kim in her Purple Worms shoes. "Young lady, come over here, please."

Kim stepped over to Miss Leslie. She looked at Sam and Jennifer suspiciously.

"Where did you get those?" Miss Leslie asked Kim.

Kim looked down at her feet, then up at Miss Leslie. "At Hulits' Shoe Store," she replied.

"What a creep!" exclaimed Jennifer. "You had to go and copy me."

"Oh, yeah?" cried Kim.

"Girls, girls! Please! This is no way for young ladies to act. I want you on your best behavior

63

from now until the end of class. Now, please go find a seat.''

Miss Leslie pointed to the folding chairs lining the ballroom.

Kim, Jennifer, and Sam turned away from each other and walked to three different sides of the room.

Oliver nervously followed Sam.

When all the students were seated, Miss Leslie stood by the piano that was in one corner of the room. She introduced herself; Mr. Pierre, her dance partner; and Miss Andrea, the pianist. Then she began reciting a list of rules for the dance class.

"Rules, rules, rules," Oliver complained to Sam.

"Jennifer is *so selfish*," Sam replied as if she hadn't heard Oliver.

"Rule number six," said Miss Leslie. "No talking while I'm speaking."

"And Kim makes me *sick*," Sam whispered.

Oliver nudged her. "*Shh*. You're going to get us in trouble."

Miss Leslie finished with the rules. Then she and Mr. Pierre demonstrated the cha-cha while Miss Andrea played the piano.

"This is an easy dance. One, two, cha-cha-cha," Miss Leslie counted aloud.

"Wow, is that stupid-looking," Sam whispered.

"Now," said Miss Leslie, "I would like the *boys* to stand up, please." Miss Leslie said *boys* loudly, as if some of the girls might get confused and stand up too.

Oliver stood up nervously.

"Boys, choose a girl and ask her to dance. The proper way for a gentleman to ask a young lady to dance is thusly: 'May I have this dance, please?' "

The boys shuffled their feet. Oliver planned to ask Sam to dance, so he wouldn't have to ask some strange girl. But he didn't want to be the first one. When he heard a boy nearby choose a partner, he said to Sam, "May I have this dance, please?"

Sam began to giggle. "Of course, your majesty."

Oliver laughed too.

"There's nothing funny about the cha-cha!" boomed Miss Leslie.

The pianist began playing again.

"One, two, cha-cha-cha," Oliver muttered as he danced with Sam.

After several minutes, Miss Leslie told the boys to change partners. Oliver looked around frantically. He was relieved to see Jennifer and Matthew not far away. "May I have this dance, please?" he asked Jennifer.

Jennifer giggled, but Matthew said rudely, "If you must!"

"Boy," said Jennifer as she cha-chaed with Oliver, "all Matthew did was complain about Josh. He wouldn't listen to me for a second. I was trying to tell him about Sam. Can you believe she gave Miss Leslie my name instead of hers—just to get me in trouble?"

"Oh, brother," said Oliver.

For half an hour, Oliver and his friends prac-

ticed the cha-cha. Soon, Oliver's feet hurt. So did his ears. Every time he danced with Kim, Jennifer, or Sam, they complained about each other. Or they complained about how the boys were complaining about each other.

Finally Miss Leslie announced a ten-minute break for polite conversation. "Sam," said Oliver, "could you please get Josh and Matthew, and meet me over here? I'll be right back."

When Oliver returned, Jennifer and Kim were with him. The six friends looked at each other angrily.

"All right," said Oliver. "Enough is enough. We're all angry, and do you know why? Rusty."

"Rusty?" repeated Sam.

"Yes, Rusty! Look at what he's doing. He's going around finding out secrets and using them to make trouble for us. He's got you three mad at one another," Oliver said, pointing to the girls. "And he's got the three of us mad at one another." Oliver indicated Josh, Matthew, and himself.

"Yeah," agreed Matthew slowly. "But why?"

"Because he's a creep," Oliver replied. "He wants to know our secret. He'll do anything to find out. But we'll show him. We won't tell. And we also won't let him get away with this! Now, what we need to do is work together."

"Unite against Rusty?" asked Josh.

"Exactly. Then we'll figure out a way to give Rusty Jackson a taste of his own medicine—or whatever it is he's got coming to him."

*   *   *

An hour later, the first dance lesson was over. Oliver, Matthew, Josh, Sam, Jennifer, and Kim were crowded into Oliver's room along with Spy. Slither had been put in the closet because Jennifer had accused the snake of "looking at her funny."

Oliver had made everybody apologize to one another, so they were all friends again.

"You know why we put up that sign?" Josh asked Oliver. "Because one weekend you were away somewhere, and we were bored without you. I didn't know what to do. So I said to Matthew, 'Wouldn't it be fun to run a business like Oliver's?' "

Josh sighed. "We had the sign up for a whole day and we didn't get any customers. Then my mom said that if we did, we would be in competition with you. I hadn't thought of that, and I didn't want to hurt you, so I took the sign down. That was the end of the dog-washing business. Only Matthew said he thought it would be better if you never found out about it."

"I should have known there was a good explanation," said Oliver. "I'm sorry I got mad."

"I'm sorry I got mad back," replied Josh. "And I'm sorry I got mad at you, Matthew."

"Me too," said Oliver.

Everybody began apologizing again. Kim, Jennifer, and Sam agreed never to wear their Purple Worms shoes to school on the same day. "We can check with each other the night before," Kim suggested.

"All right," said Oliver, "what we have to do now is get even with Rusty. We have to plan the *worst possible punishment* for him. And I know just what to do."

CHAPTER
7

Oliver explained the plan to his friends.

"I got the idea this afternoon. I found out that there's another dance class at Miss Leslie's. It's held at the same time as ours. But it's for older kids. We're the junior class and they're the senior class."

"Where is it held?" asked Sam. She looked puzzled.

"Upstairs," replied Oliver. "There's another ballroom right above ours. The teacher for the seniors is Miss Pamela, Miss Leslie's daughter. And she's taller and meaner and uglier than Miss Leslie."

"Perfect!" said Josh. He rubbed his hands together.

"Do you all know the plan?" asked Oliver.

His friends nodded.

"Matthew and I are in charge of printing fliers," said Josh.

"Jennifer and I are in charge of delivering them," said Kim.

"Right," said Oliver. "And Sam and I will take care of ferret-training."

Oliver and his friends were very busy the next day. Sam went over to the Moffitts' house right after school.

"We'd better get started," she said.

"Right," agreed Oliver.

"How are we ever going to teach him to sneak things out of a knapsack?" asked Sam. "That seems awfully hard. When you say, 'Bring me,' doesn't he bring things from any old place?"

"Yes," said Oliver, "but—what if Spy thought that all knapsacks had Cracker Jacks inside? He'd go straight into every knapsack he could find, right?"

"Oh, I see," said Sam slowly.

"That's why I wanted you to bring your knapsack today. Now," Oliver went on, "we'll go into the living room. My knapsack's on the couch. You put yours on that table."

Sam laid her knapsack down.

"Okay," said Oliver. "A few Cracker Jacks, and we're all set." He emptied several Cracker Jacks into each knapsack. Then he ran upstairs, got Spy out of his cage, and returned to the living room.

"Want a treat?" Oliver asked Spy.

He held the ferret up to the knapsacks and showed him the Cracker Jacks inside. Spy's nose wrinkled and twitched like crazy. Oliver pulled him away and carried him to a corner of the room.

"Bring me!" he said to Spy.

Spy rippled across the floor. He made a beeline for the knapsacks. He could hardly decide which one to try first. At last he scurried into Sam's. He burrowed right under the flap. Only his tail showed. It hung outside the knapsack, twitching back and forth.

Crunch, crunch.

"He has to eat the Cracker Jacks first!" said Sam with a giggle.

Crunch, crunch.

Oliver grew impatient.

"Spy, bring me," he reminded the ferret.

Spy's tail disappeared inside the knapsack. A moment later, two dark eyes peered out from under the flap. Spy poked his head through. Then he zipped back to Oliver. He dropped an eraser shaped like a strawberry at his feet.

"Good boy!" cried Oliver. "Now," he said to Sam, "we'll do it again."

Oliver turned Spy around. "Bring me," he said again.

This time, Spy ran for Oliver's knapsack. After he ate the Cracker Jacks, he brought Oliver a pencil.

"But what if there are no Cracker Jacks in Rusty's knapsack?" asked Sam. "Or worse, what if he doesn't bring his knapsack?"

"Oh, I'm sure he'll bring it," Oliver replied. "He's Mr. Photographer now, remember? That's where he carries his film and camera. As for the Cracker Jacks ... well, I'll bet he *will* have a supply, but even if he doesn't, Spy will be sure to go into the knapsack anyway. He wouldn't want to pass up a chance for a treat. Wait, let's try something. I'll take Spy out of the room. You move the knapsacks around. But this time, don't put any Cracker Jacks inside."

"Okay," said Sam.

Several moments later, Oliver brought Spy back to the living room. Sam's knapsack was on the floor by a chair. Oliver's was on a footstool.

"Bring me!" said Oliver.

Spy made a mad dash for Sam's knapsack and returned with her assignment pad.

"See?" said Oliver.

"Amazing," replied Sam. She grinned. "Look out, Rusty Jackson!"

Meanwhile, Josh and Matthew were busy working on Josh's computer.

"How does this sound?" asked Josh as he typed away. " 'Learn refinement. Improve your manners. Learn to be light on your feet. Come to Miss Leslie's Dance Studio for Young Ladies and Gentlemen.' "

"Gag, barf. It sounds great," said Matthew. "Remember, we have to say where the classes are. And when. And the phone number to call."

"Right," said Josh. "I was just getting to that part."

"How about this?" asked Matthew. " 'Don't be a wallflower at life's party!' "

Josh laughed. "That's really gross! I love it! How many fliers do you think we should make?"

"Oh, about four. Remember, they're going only to Rusty's house. We don't want to give the Jacksons too many. They'll get suspicious. Jennifer and Kim can put one up on that telephone pole in front of the Jacksons'. They can put another on the big tree by the sidewalk. Then they can put the last two in the Jacksons' mailbox. One today, one tomorrow. That ought to do the trick."

Josh nodded. He typed a few more words. He began to smile. " 'Learn to trot like a fox,' " he read. " 'Learn to cha-cha your troubles away. Learn how to dance with a girl who wears little white gloves. Yes, folks, you, too, can be a nerd.' "

"Or just look like one," added Matthew.

Josh began typing again. The boys were still laughing when Kim and Jennifer rang Josh's doorbell.

"What's so funny?" asked Jennifer.

"This," said Josh. He held out a flier.

" 'Learn to be a nerd,' " read Jennifer. " 'Do you have slicked-back hair? Do you wear highly polished shoes and conservative ties? Then come to Miss Leslie's Dance Studio for Young Ladies and Gentlemen. You'll fit right in.' " Jennifer's eyes opened wide. "Josh! Matthew!" she cried. "Are you kidding?"

"That'll never work!" added Kim.

"Oh, calm down," said Matthew. "Of course we're kidding. It's a *joke*!"

"Yeah, we just got a little carried away." Josh couldn't stop laughing.

"Here," said Matthew. "These are the real fliers. Put one up on the tree in front of Rusty's house, put another on that telephone pole, and put the third in the mailbox. The last one is for tomorrow. Put it in their mailbox late in the morning. The Jacksons will think the letter carrier delivered it."

"Right," said Kim.

"Got it," said Jennifer.

On Saturday morning, Oliver slept late. He took his time getting up. First he lay in bed reading a book about reptiles. Then he got out of bed and wandered into the TV room. He watched cartoons. Finally he got dressed.

"Mmm, breakfast time," said Oliver, heading into the kitchen.

He poured himself a huge bowl of Choco-Dots. He raised his spoon, and—

Ding-dong.

"Sheesh," said Oliver. "Mom, can you get that?"

"Oliver, can you get that?" Mrs. Moffitt was yelling at the same time.

Oliver heaved a sigh. His mouth was watering for Choco-Dots. But he answered the door.

"Oliver! Oliver! It worked!"

Kim and Jennifer were on the Moffitts' front

porch. Both of them were jumping up and down and screaming.

"What worked?" asked Oliver.

"Our plan!" replied Jennifer. "We didn't even have to put the last flier in the Jacksons' mailbox."

"You mean . . . ?" said Oliver.

Kim nodded. "That's right. We were just about to put the flier in the box—"

"We had the box open and everything," added Jennifer smugly.

"—when the front door to Rusty's house opened and he came out yelling, 'I will not take dancing lessons! I will not! You call that Miss Leslie back and say you changed your mind!' "

"And then," Jennifer continued, "Mrs. Jackson said she would do no such thing. She said, 'Rusty, we're going to go downtown right now. We've got to get you some new ties. You're starting dancing school on Monday.' "

"All right!" exclaimed Oliver. "That's perfect. Our next lesson is on Monday too."

"Will Spy be ready?" asked Kim.

"No problem," Oliver replied. "We'll just put in a little more practice time."

Oliver was not the only one in the Moffitt house who had to go to Miss Leslie's on Monday.

"Are you ready, Spy?" Oliver asked the ferret. "I hope so. You've got to do your trick today or I'm a dead duck. Your family's coming home soon, and you'll have to go back to them."

Spy turned himself into an upside-down *U* and hopped up and down.

"Okay, okay," said Oliver. "Don't get too excited."

When Oliver left the house, he still looked like a nerd. But this time he was carrying Spy's cage. He had covered it with a light blanket.

"The only tricky part," Oliver told his friends when he met them outside the dance studio, "will be getting this cage into the coat room."

"We'll surround you, Oliver," said Matthew. "Keep the cage low. I think it will work. Hey, do you have Spy's leash?"

"It's in my pocket."

"Good."

The kids waited until the rest of the students began to file into Miss Leslie's. Then Josh, Matthew, Kim, and Jennifer bunched around Oliver and Spy. They hustled into the coat room on the first floor and buried Spy's cage under their sweaters and jackets.

"It's only for a minute," Oliver whispered to the ferret. "Now you guys go on ahead," he told his friends. "I'll just have to tell Miss Leslie I was late or something."

Oliver hid in a closet until he could hear the dance classes beginning. Then he clipped on Spy's leash and dashed upstairs. Outside the coat room for the senior class, Oliver let Spy loose.

"Bring me," he whispered.

Oliver couldn't go into the coat room himself. If he got caught rifling through somebody's knap-

sack, he'd be in big trouble. But no one would notice the little ferret.

Oliver stood in the hallway. He pretended he was waiting to use the boys' room.

"Spy," he whispered. "I hope you really learned your new trick."

CHAPTER
8

By the time dance class was over, Oliver was in a great mood. "I did it!" he exclaimed to Sam as they walked home with Spy.

"I can't believe it!" Sam replied. "Now you've got just what you need to blackmail Rusty."

"I wonder why he didn't say anything to me about Slither yet," said Oliver. "It's not like Rusty to forget one of his nasty plans. And today's the deadline. He said he'd tell my mom about Slither if we didn't let him in on our secret by today. But he hasn't said a word to me."

"He's probably too mad about Miss Leslie's," said Sam gleefully.

"Yeah," agreed Oliver with a grin. "When I peeked in on his class, he sure looked unhappy. His partner was saying, 'One, two, cha-cha-cha,' and every time she said the second 'cha' she stepped on Rusty's foot."

They had reached Sam's house. "Well, I'd better go in," said Sam. "I want to get these horrible black shoes off my feet."

"Do you want to say good-bye to Spy?" asked Oliver. "I have to return both him and Slither before Mom comes home."

"Sure," replied Sam. She knelt by Spy's cage. "Good-bye, little Spy. You sure were a lot of fun."

"And useful," added Oliver.

"I'll say. See you, Oliver."

" 'Bye, Sam."

Oliver took Spy into his house and set his cage in his room. He changed out of his dancing class clothes. He even remembered to empty his pants pockets—four pennies, a stick of gum, a baseball card, Spy's leash, and a secret little envelope that he hid in his dresser drawer.

"Okay, Slither old boy," he said to the snake. "You're going home now. Spy, I'll be back for you in a while."

Oliver carried Slither's cage out of his house and down the street. He returned him to his owner, who happily paid Oliver five dollars. As Oliver walked back to his house, he thought, "That was close. I can't believe I sat for Slither all that time and Mom didn't find out. With any luck, she'll never know. I just hope our plan w—"

Oliver stopped walking. His thoughts had been interrupted by a horrible sight.

Rusty Jackson was seated on the Moffitts' front steps. His feet were crossed in front of him. He was whistling. He looked very sure of himself.

"Oh, there you are, Moffitt," said Rusty. He yawned and got to his feet.

Oliver shivered. He walked across his yard and faced Rusty.

Rusty made a big show of checking his watch. "Hmm," he said. "About time for your mommy to come home, isn't it, Moffitt?"

"Oh, you think you're so smart," said Oliver. "But I just gave Slither back to his owner. He's gone. Mom never saw him."

Rusty shrugged. "Makes no difference to me. All I have to do is show her one little photo, and she'll know a snake was living in her house. Right down the hall from her bedroom . . ."

Oliver stood his ground.

"Okay, so what's the secret?" asked Rusty.

"I'm not telling," replied Oliver.

Rusty looked surprised, but only for a moment. He dangled the photo in front of Oliver. "Tell me the secret."

"No."

"Tell me!"

"No!"

"Tell me!"

"No!"

"TELL ME!"

"All right," said Oliver.

"All right?" asked Rusty. "You're going to tell?"

"Yes. But first I have to get something. I'll be right back."

"Sure. No problem," said Rusty. "Oh, Moffitt," he added. "You're such a pushover."

"Yeah, well . . ."

Oliver went into his house and up to his room. He took the envelope out of his drawer and ran back to Rusty with it.

"What's that?" asked Rusty.

"It's part of the secret. Maybe you'd like to work out a little trade."

"Huh?"

"My picture for yours," said Oliver.

Oliver opened the envelope. He pulled out a photo. The photo showed Rusty—in his dance class, waltzing around with some girl. The girl was very pretty. She had long silky hair that fell over her shoulders. And she was looking into Rusty's eyes as if she'd just fallen in love with him.

Rusty looked from the photo to Oliver.

"Gertrude Schweinfleisch!" he exclaimed.

"Oh, is that who she is?" asked Oliver. "I was wondering."

"What—wh—who?" Rusty spluttered.

"What was that?" said Oliver. "I didn't quite catch what you said."

"Where did you get that?" Rusty managed to ask.

"I took it myself. With your camera."

"You mean," said Rusty, turning pale, "you were at Miss Leslie's today?"

"That's right," was all Oliver replied. There

was no reason for Rusty to know why Oliver had been at Miss Leslie's. Not yet anyway.

"But how did you know I'd be there?"

"Oh, I have my ways."

"And, hey!" shouted Rusty. "How did you get my camera, you little thief?"

"I did not take your camera," said Oliver. He paused. "Spy did."

"Spy did!"

"Yup."

"How?" Rusty demanded.

"He's a very smart little ferret," said Oliver. "He learns easily. He knows lots of tricks. And one of them is retrieving things out of knapsacks. He took your camera out of your knapsack. I used your camera to take that picture. It was really a snap, Rusty!"

"My camera! You thief! You're a thief, Oliver Moffitt. I ought to haul you down to the police station and have you arrested!"

"You do, and I'll tell everyone that you have to take lessons at Miss Leslie's Dance Studio for Young Ladies and Gentlemen. I'm sure you'd like all your friends to know that."

"Why you little—"

"And," Oliver continued, ignoring Rusty, "if you ever show that picture of Slither and me to Mom, I'll show this picture of Gertrude and you to Betsy Hardy."

"You wouldn't dare."

"Yes, I would," said Oliver calmly. "So how about that trade?"

"My picture for yours?"

"And all the negatives."

Rusty sighed loudly. "I don't have them with me, but I'll trade you tomorrow in school."

"Okay," said Oliver. "By the way, if you happen to 'forget' to bring them tomorrow, this photo will wind up on Betsy Hardy's desk."

"Okay, okay, okay." Rusty walked off.

As soon as he was out of sight, Oliver packed up Spy's things carefully. Then he put Spy's leash on and walked him back to the Sawyers' house.

"Hi, Spy!" said Scott when he answered the door.

Spy jumped up and down, up and down. He scrambled up Scott's pants. He let Scott hold him on his back and rub his tummy.

"Gosh," said Oliver, "he sure is glad to see you."

"I guess so," replied Scott. "Come on inside. You can put Spy's things right here in the hall."

Oliver stepped through the doorway. He unloaded Spy's cage and food and litter in a heap.

"Hey!" called a voice from the kitchen. "Is Spy here?"

"Yup," replied Scott. "Come see him."

Jimmy Sawyer ran into the hall. He was wearing a hat with a pair of Mickey Mouse ears on it. "Hey, Spy!" He stuck out his hand and clucked his tongue. "Say hello."

From his lazy position, lolling on his back, Spy stuck out one of his front paws for Jimmy to shake.

"Good boy!" said Jimmy. He gave Spy a Cracker Jack.

"Wow," said Oliver. "I didn't know he could do that."

"It works when you're leaving too," added Scott. "Just say 'Say good-bye' instead."

Oliver waited until he had been paid and was ready to leave. Then he sat on the floor by the ferret. He stuck his hand out. "Say good-bye," he said.

Spy stuck one paw out and Oliver shook it.

" 'Bye, Spy. You were a great pet."

Spy smiled and chattered.

"By the way," Oliver called over his shoulder, "if you have a knapsack, put it someplace where Spy can see it, and then say, 'Bring me.' You'll be surprised."

The next day, when school was over, Oliver and his friends waited for Rusty Jackson at the bicycle racks.

"What if he doesn't show up?" said Oliver nervously.

But sure enough, Rusty sauntered over to Oliver a few moments later.

"I see you brought all your little friends along," he said.

"Yeah. They wanted to be in on the occasion. Admit it, Rusty. I got you. I got you good."

Rusty scowled.

"Where's the picture, Jackson?" Oliver demanded.

"It's here. It's here."

Rusty held it out.

Oliver held his picture out.

Matthew stepped forward. He swapped the photos and the negatives.

Without a word, Rusty turned. He walked away, shaking his head. "I never even found out the secret," he muttered.

Oliver and his friends grinned at one another. Next week, there was going to be a joint dance lesson. For the first time, the junior and senior dance classes would meet each other. Rusty would finally find out the big secret. But it would be too late. It would be a secret *he'd* have to keep too!